Nobody's Dog

Charlotte Graeber

Illustrated by Barry Root

Hyperion Books for Children
New York

1567 8012

For Troy Andrew
and Sparky the Wonder Dog—C. G.

For Marjorie Stephenson Drewry—B. R.

Text © 1998 by Charlotte Graeber.
Illustrations © 1998 by Barry Root.

Printed in Singapore.

First Edition
1 3 5 7 9 10 8 6 4 2

The artwork for this book is prepared using watercolor and gouache on Arches paper.
The text for this book is set in 14-point Goudy.

Library of Congress Cataloging-in-Publication Data

Graeber, Charlotte Towner.
Nobody's Dog / Charlotte Graeber ; illustrated by Barry Root—1st ed.
p.   cm.
Summary: After he is abandoned on River Road, Nobody's Dog uses his persistence to
find a home.
ISBN 0-7868-0109-3 (trade)—ISBN 0-7868-2093-4 (lib. hdg.)
[1. Dogs—Fiction.] I. Root, Barry, ill. II. Title.
PZ7.G75153N1   1998
[E]—dc21   97-25632

Nobody's Dog

$\mathcal{N}$obody on River Road wanted the dog. One night someone stopped their car for a moment and then sped away—leaving behind

the small white dog with one brown ear
(the right one), two brown paws (the front
ones), and a feathery tail.

Mr. Fitz did not want the dog. "He's too small," he told his wife. And his wife agreed. The Fitzes liked things big. They had a big house, a big car, and big appetites. And the

dog was almost as small as Mrs. Applegate's
cat next door.

"Maybe Mrs. Applegate will take him in,"
Mrs. Fitz said.

   Mrs. Applegate did not want the dog. "He's too
noisy," she told her cat. They lived in a quiet
house. Even the cat's purr was quiet. And the small
dog's bark was as noisy as the Swanson children
banging their screen door across the street.

   "Maybe the Swansons will take in the poor
thing," Mrs. Applegate said.

The Swanson children *did* want the dog! "He's so small! He's so cute! Can we keep him?" all three asked.

"No more pets! Enough is enough!" their parents said. The Swansons already had three cats, two canaries, four gerbils, a rabbit, a mouse, a guinea pig, five hamsters, and a large dog.

"Maybe Miss Pepper will take him in," Mrs. Swanson said.

Miss Pepper didn't have any pets, but she *did* have her lovely garden. She had fenced it in to keep the Swansons' dog out. She did not want a dog of any size ruining her precious flowers. She did not want the small white dog with one brown ear (the right one), two brown paws (the front ones), and a feathery tail.

And so the small dog sat watching the road.

Mr. and Mrs. Fitz watched the dog watching the road.

"He's waiting for his owner," Mrs. Fitz said.

"He must be thirsty," Mr. Fitz said. And, although he did not want the small dog, he set out a big pail of water.

Mrs. Applegate and her cat watched the dog watching the road, and, although she did not want the noisy dog, she placed a bowl of Kitty Krunchies on her porch.

The dog was hungry. He ate until his tummy bulged like a small balloon.

The Swanson children felt sorry for the small dog. "Poor little dog. He must be lonely," they said. They picked him up and carried him into their crowded house. "Please, please, can we keep him?" they begged their mother.

"No! No! No!" she said more firmly than before.

The Swanson dog growled. The Swanson cats hissed. The small dog jumped out of the children's arms.

Through the screen door and around the corner he ran!

Under Miss Pepper's garden gate he squeezed his small self.

Miss Pepper was not at home. She had gone out to purchase a new pair of garden gloves. When she returned she found the small dog curled up and fast asleep in her petunias.

"Oh no!" Miss Pepper cried. "My petunias!"

The small dog woke up. And fast as a fox he raced back under the gate with Miss Pepper close behind. "Stay out of my garden," she scolded.

Miss Pepper's petunias were not broken—only flattened a bit. Still, she did not want the dog in her garden. She would find a way to keep him out!

And she did! She rolled a stone against the garden gate.

The small white dog sat watching. He liked Miss Pepper's garden. It smelled nice. He would find a way to get back in.

And he did! He waited until dusk, when Miss
Pepper went inside. Then he dug, dug, dug. The
dirt flew.

The stone came loose. And under the gate the
small dog squeezed his small self once again.

The next morning Miss Pepper found the dog under her snowball bush. "You are an impossible pest!" she scolded. "Don't you understand? I don't want you in my garden."

The dog barked a small bark and hurried back under the gate.

Miss Pepper kept bags of potting soil next to her garage. One after another she carried them to the gate and stacked them firmly across the opening. Maybe the bags would keep the small dog out.

The small dog watched with his feathery tail wagging. He watched until Miss Pepper left the garden.

Then he pulled at the bags with his teeth. He shoved at them with his nose. He pulled and shoved until the bags wobbled. He pulled and shoved until they tumbled and fell. And back under the gate he went.

Miss Pepper was watching. This time she
waited until the dog settled himself under the

snowball bush. She waited
until he was fast asleep. Then
she tiptoed out and scooped
him up.

"You are worse than a
weed," she said firmly. "Popping
up where you are not wanted."

The small dog nuzzled
under her chin. But Miss Pepper set him
down firmly on the other side of the fence.

"You are a smart little rascal,"
she said. "But I do not want you
in my garden."

The small dog did not move. He sat watching the gate and Miss Pepper. He was determined to get back in.

Miss Pepper was determined to keep the small dog out.

Miss Pepper placed her sprinkler next to the gate. She turned on the sprinkler and waited behind the house.

The small dog did not hesitate. As soon as Miss Pepper was out of sight he squeezed under the gate. Quick as a rabbit he dashed through the water. He looked quite joyful as he shook himself off.

Miss Pepper collapsed onto her garden swing. "You are a scamp!" she said. "What am I going to do with you?"

The small white dog moved closer. Around the petunias, past the snowball bush, up to the swing he came.

And there he sat, holding up one paw.

Miss Pepper sighed.

The dog wagged his feathery tail.

Miss Pepper did not want a dog in her garden. But she took the small dog's paw and said, "How do you do?"

To Miss Pepper's surprise, the dog leaped onto the swing—turned around twice—and settled himself on her lap.

Miss Pepper had never owned a dog. She had never fed, cuddled, played with, patted, or petted a dog in her whole life.

But she began to pet the small dog's ears. "I wonder if I could teach a small dog to stay out of my flowers," she said.

The small dog nudged her arm with his small black nose.

Miss Pepper's heart felt full as a bucket. She would give it a try.

"*I* will buy you dog food and a collar," she told the dog. "*You* will have to mind your manners in my garden." She set the dog down and started towards the house.

Across the way Mr. and Mrs. Fitz cheered a big "Hoorah!"

Mrs. Applegate stroked her cat and said, "Good," in a quiet voice. The Swanson children clapped their hands.

They all knew that the small, white, brown-eared (the right one), brown-pawed (the front ones), feathery-tailed, nobody's dog was Miss Pepper's dog now!